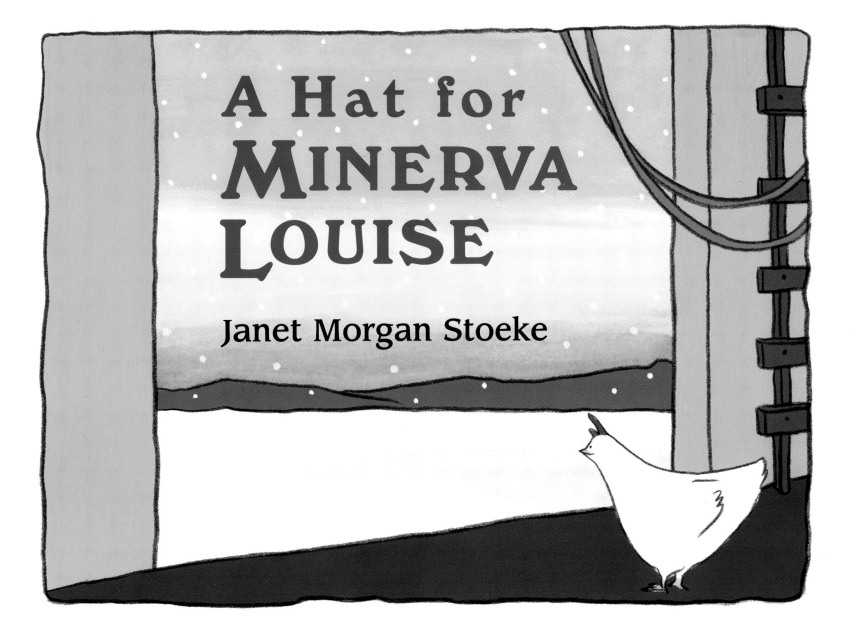

A Hat for
MINERVA
LOUISE

Janet Morgan Stoeke

■

For Colin Wilcox Brooks

■

Library of Congress Cataloging-in-Publication Data
Stoeke, Janet Morgan.
A hat for Minerva Louise /by Janet Morgan Stoeke.—1st ed.
p. cm.
Summary: Minerva Louise, a snow-loving chicken, mistakes
a pair of mittens for two hats to keep both ends warm.
ISBN 1-58048-165-5
(1. Chickens—Fiction. 2. Hats—Fiction.) 1. Title.
PZ7.S8696Hat 1994 (E)—dc20 94-2139 CIP AC

Published in the United States 1994 by Dutton Children's Books,
a division of Penguin Books USA Inc.
375 Hudson Street, New York, New York 10014
Printed in Hong Kong
First Edition
5 7 9 10 8 6

Minerva Louise loved snowy mornings.

Her friends didn't like them one bit.

They stayed inside all day with their heads tucked under their wings.

Not Minerva Louise. She couldn't
wait to go out exploring.

Everything was so beautiful!

She wanted to stay out all day.
But it was too cold.

If I had some warm things like you,
she said, I could stay out and play.

A scarf might help.

But not this one. It's way too big.

And these shoes are too big, too.

A hat! That's just what I need.

But not this one.

And not this one, either.
It's too heavy.

There must be a hat around
here somewhere.

Minerva Louise looked outside.
Everyone had on a fluffy white hat!

Oh, *your* hat is wonderful!
Where did you get it?

Oh, look! What's over here?

A hat! It's perfect. But what's this?

Oh, it's two hats!

Which was just fine

with Minerva Louise.